Grandma's TINY HOUSE

A Counting Story!

JaNay Brown-Wood illustrated by Priscilla Burris

Charlesbridge

To my grandma, Mary Richardson,
and to my big, wonderful family
for their unrelenting love and support!
—J. B-W.

For ALL lovable grandmas, and especially for
Lily, Harriet, Isabel, Rosario, Judy, and Blanche!
—P. B.

First paperback edition 2021
Text copyright © 2017 by JaNay Brown-Wood
Illustrations copyright © 2017 by Priscilla Burris

Published by Charlesbridge
9 Galen Street, Watertown, MA 02472
(617) 926-0329 · www.charlesbridge.com

Library of Congress Cataloging-in-Publication Data
Names: Brown-Wood, JaNay, author. | Burris, Priscilla, illustrator.
Title: Grandma's tiny house / JaNay Brown-Wood; illustrated by Priscilla Burris.
Description: Watertown, MA: Charlesbridge, [2016] | Summary: In rhyming text,
    when the whole family and guests show up for the big dinner at Grandma's house,
    it becomes clear that the house is much too small to hold them all.
Identifiers: LCCN 2016024031 (print) | LCCN 2016025261 (ebook)
    | ISBN 9781580897129 (reinforced for library use) | ISBN 9781623543051 (paperback)
    | ISBN 9781607348689 (ebook) | ISBN 9781607348696 (ebook pdf)
Subjects: LCSH: Stories in rhyme. | Family life—Juvenile fiction. | Holidays—Juvenile
    fiction. | Food—Juvenile fiction. | Grandmothers—Juvenile fiction. | Counting. |
    CYAC: Stories in rhyme. | Family life—Fiction. | Holidays—Fiction. | Food—Fiction.
    | Grandmothers—Fiction. | Counting.
Classification: LCC PZ8.3.B81577 Gr 2016 (print) | LCC PZ8.3.B81577 (ebook)
    | DDC [E]—dc23
LC record available at https://lccn.loc.gov/2016024031

Printed in China
(hc) 10 9 8 7 6 5 4 3
(pb) 10 9 8 7 6 5 4 3 2 1

Illustrations created in Photoshop
Display type set in Wanderlust Shine by Cultivated Mind
Text type set in Carrotflower by Font Diner
Color separations by Colourscan Print Co Pte Ltd, Singapore
Printed by 1010 Printing International Limited in Huizhou, Guangdong, China
Production supervision by Brian G. Walker and Jennifer Most Delaney
Designed by Diane M. Earley

with SIX dozen biscuits and jam made of pears.

with EIGHT jugs of lemonade, ice-cold and fine.

NINE chatting aunties all head for the den,
and set down the cheesecakes that add up to TEN.

ELEVEN nephews join, slapping high-fives

and fumbling TWELVE sweet-potato pies.

THIRTEEN thrilled nieces burst in on the scene,

And who is that running? Last but not least,
FIFTEEN hungry grandkids stampede to the feast.

That's when the walls bulge. There is no more space!

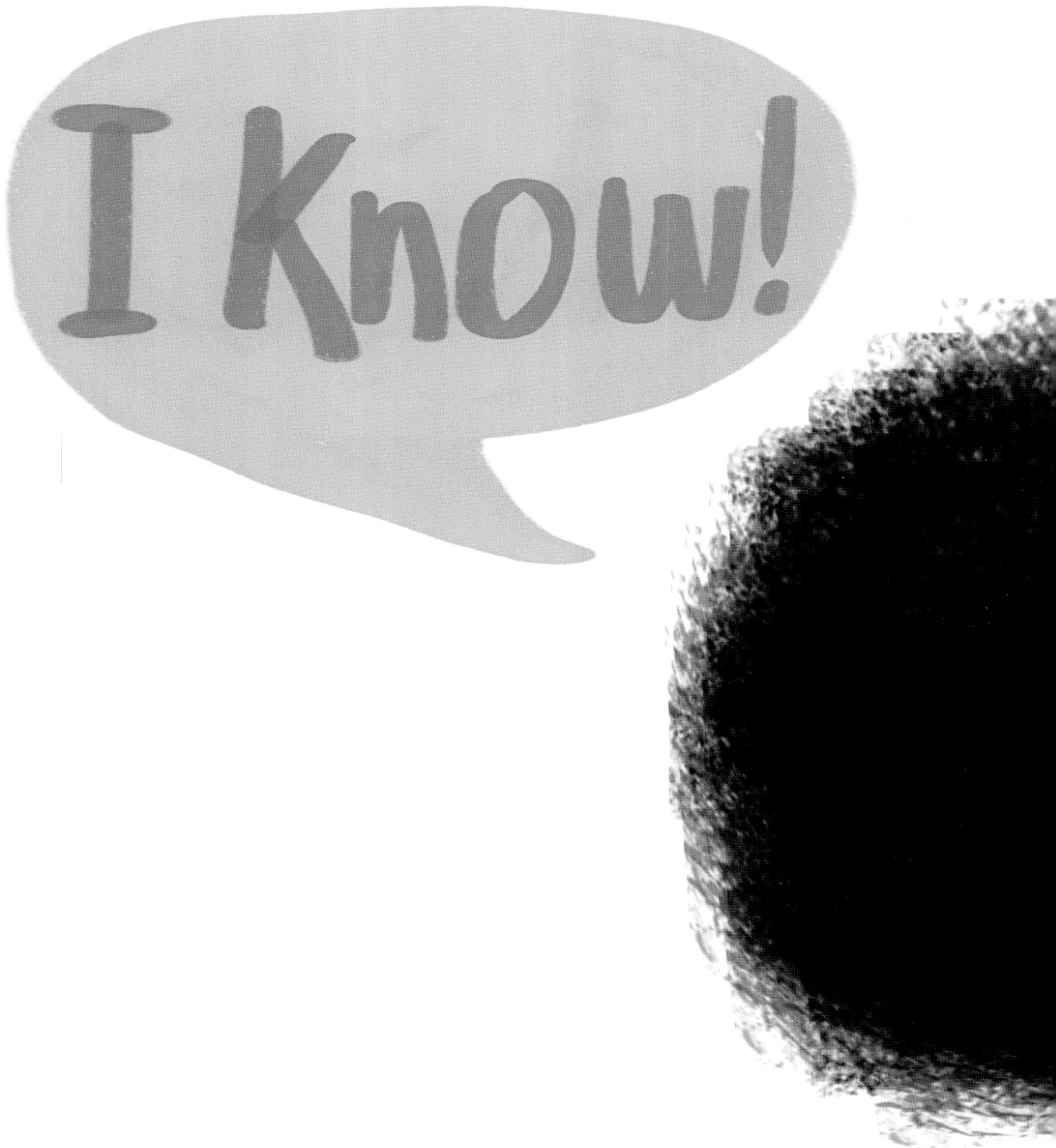
I Know!

Why don't we move our big dinner outside?"

So out skip the neighbors, nephews, and nieces,

The rest bring the food
down Grandma's back stairs.

Perfect in size, at the edge
of Brown Street,

sits Grandma's backyard, where we all go to EAT.